DATE DUE

DEC 2 6 1996		
MAI JUL 27 1996		
NOV 2 1 1996		
MAI FEB 06 1997		
FEB 07 1998	AUG 2 2 1997	
MAI JUL 24 1997		

Roller Coaster

by Kevin O'Malley

You have to be Taller than my NOSE!

Lothrop, Lee & Shepard Books · New York

First Edition 1 2 3 4 5 6 7 8 9 10
Library of Congress Cataloging in Publication Data
was not available in time for the publication of this book,
but can be obtained from the Library of Congress.
Roller Coaster. ISBN 0-688-13971-X. ISBN 0-688-13972-8 (lib bdg.)
Library of Congress Catalog Card Number: 94 -79123.
The illustrations in this book were done in acrylic paints,pen and ink, and colored pencils on water
color paper. The display and text type were set in Souvenir Separations by Blacktone Graphics.
Printed by Berryville Graphics. Production supervision by Bonnie King.

For Mary Kate

Get your PORTRAIT Drawn

— By —
Kevin O'Malley

Last year, when we went to Fantasy Park,

it was awesome.

I played putt-putt golf

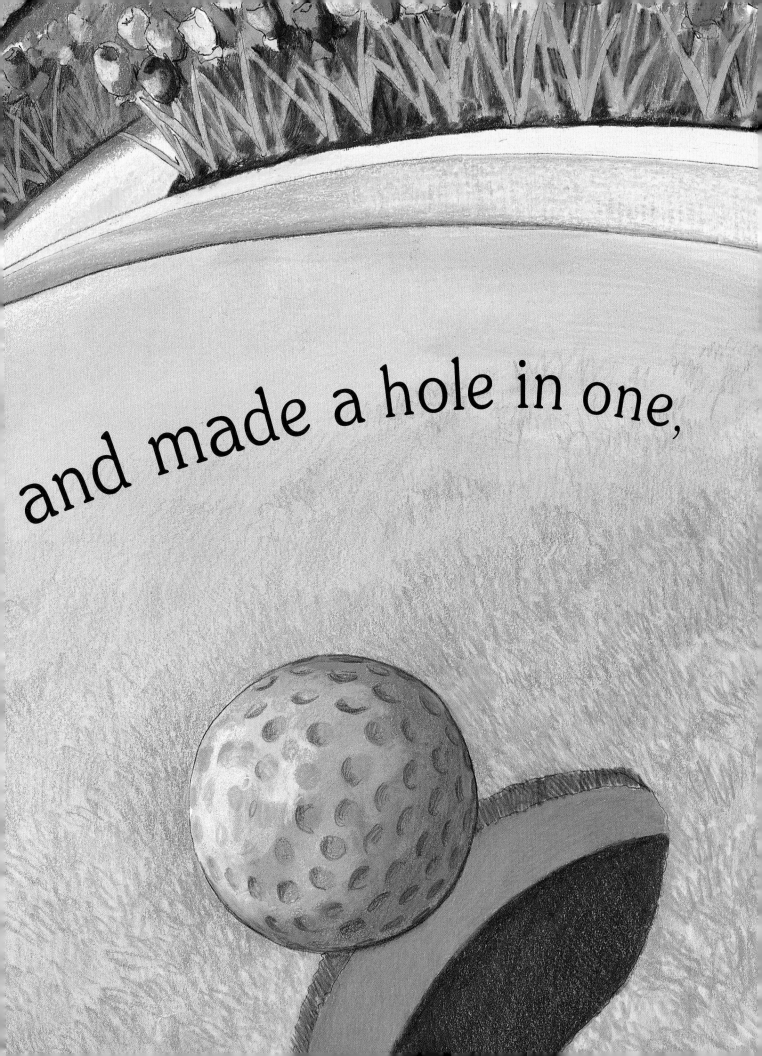

and made a hole in one,

and ate a triple-dip ice-cream

cone with sprinkles.

I got a pair of sunglasses

and a **really** cool T-shirt,

and **laughed** and **laughed**

in the **fun house.**

I won a big prize at

the ring-toss booth,

and got to go on

all the rides...

...except the roller coaster.

The man said I was too *short.*

I'm big enough to ride...

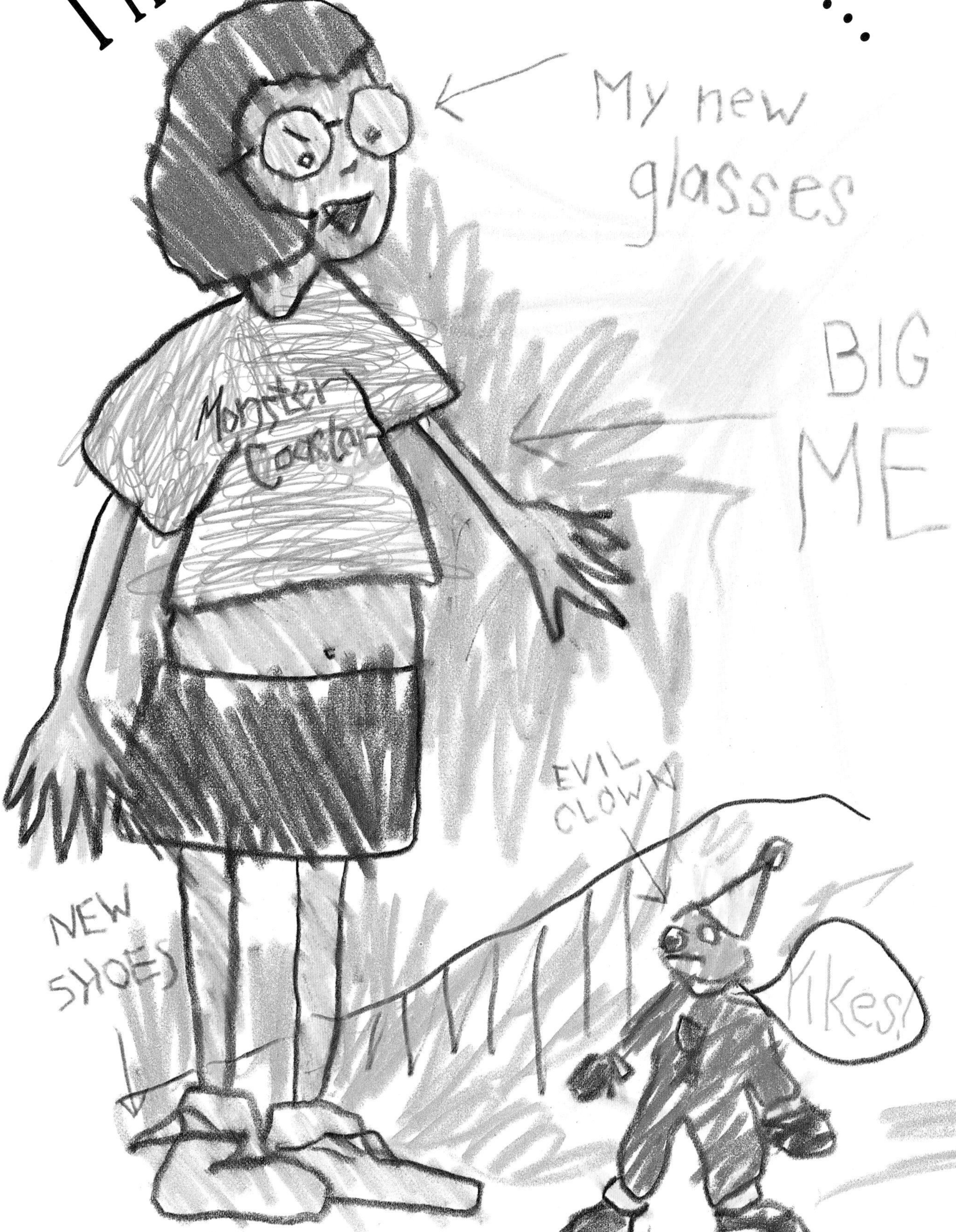

THE ROLLER